Hurry, Hurry, Mary Dear

Hurry, Hurry, Mary Dear

by

N. M. Bodecker

Illustrated by Erik Blegvad

SIMON AND SCHUSTER • LONDON

N. M. Bodecker's drawing in a letter congratulating Lenore and Erik Blegvad
on the birth of their son, Peter, in 1951.

*

SIMON AND SCHUSTER

First published in Great Britain in 2004 by
Simon and Schuster UK Ltd, Africa House, 64–78 Kingsway, London WC2B 6AH.

Originally published in the USA in 1998 by Margaret K. McElderry Books,
an imprint of Simon & Schuster Children's Publishing Division,
1230 Avenue of the Americas,
New York, NY 10020.

Book design by Michael Nelson.

The text of this book was set in Janson.
The illustrations were rendered in watercolour.

ISBN 0689 86122-2

Printed in China
First Edition
1 3 5 7 10 8 6 4 2

FOREWORD BY THE ILLUSTRATOR

This domestic drama was composed by my friend Bo, or N. M. Bodecker as he is known, in 1975 when he was still hale and hearty. Well, he never was completely that, not even in the Copenhagen Art School where we met in 1941. Like many witty people he was often moody and morose. Illustrating my friend's poem now, I find myself smiling at the many funny things Bo wrote, drew, said and did. For example, the fierce competitions he invented, not for any favours from girlfriends or praise from teachers, but to see which of us could grow the largest moustache or get to Paris first. We were not inseparable, but, oddly enough, we were together at many of the century's momentous events. After World War II, we both married American college graduates we had met in Paris. We were both commercial artists and both emigrated to the United States, where we opened a studio in Westport, Connecticut. Here we worked for many years and played and competed. Of course we also spoke Danish all day. And it was here that Bo began writing his so-called nonsense poems in English. He illustrated them with the most delightful pen and ink drawings. Bo was a superb illustrator. My illustrations here are based on Bo's, but I'm afraid my heroine is only a pale imitation of his. It can't be helped. After all, I'm not the same as I was when I shared that studio with my friend Bo. He died in 1988 in his beloved New England. Trying to draw his Mary has put me in touch with Bo again, but my Danish is getting rusty.

E.B.

London, November 1997

Hurry, hurry, Mary dear,
fall is over, winter's here.

Not a moment to be lost,
in a minute we get frost!

In an hour we get snow!
Drifts like houses! Ten below!

Pick the apples,

dill the pickles,

chop down the trees for wooden nickels.

Dig the turnips,

split the peas,

cook molasses,

curdle cheese.

Churn the butter,

smoke the hams,

can tomatoes,

put up jams.

Stack the stove wood,

string the beans,

up the storms
and down the screens.

Pull the curtains,
close the shutters.
Dreadfully the wild wind
mutters.

Oil the snowshoes,

stoke the fires.
Soon the roads are hopeless mires.

Mend the mittens, knit the sweaters,

bring my glasses, mail my letters.

Toast the muffins, brew the tea,
hot and sweet and good for me.

Bake me doughnuts, plain and frosted...

What, my dear? You feel exhausted?

Mary dear.